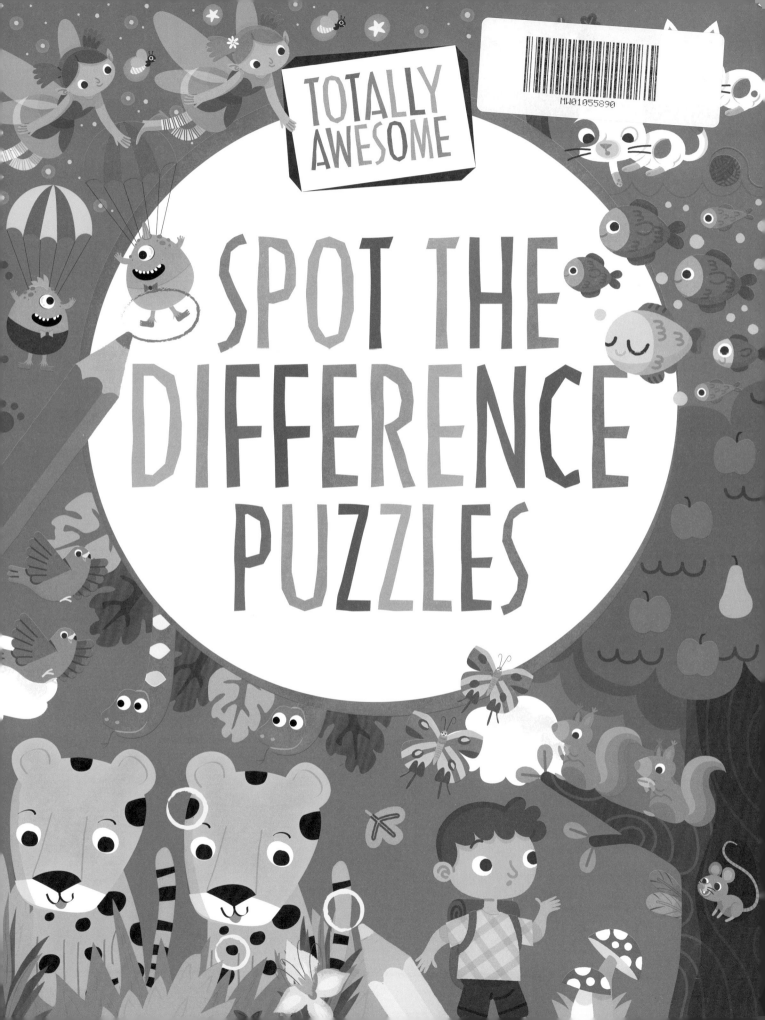

TOTALLY
AWESOME

SPOT THE DIFFERENCE PUZZLES

First published 2017 by Parragon Books, Ltd.

Copyright © 2021 Cottage Door Press, LLC
5005 Newport Drive, Rolling Meadows, Illinois 60008

Illustrated by Beatrice Costamagna, Tim Budgen,
AndoTwin, and Isabel Aniel

ISBN: 978-1-64638-021-3

www.cottagedoorpress.com

TOTALLY
AWESOME

SPOT THE DIFFERENCE PUZZLES

cottage door press®

Balloon Race
Up, up, and away!

Find **8** differences in this picture before the balloons float away!

famous or fake?

Vincent van Cough has copied some famous works of art. His paintings on the right are all terrible fakes! Circle **1** mistake in each fake.

Someone's been snacking at the birthday feast before the guests have arrived.

Happy

Birthday

Can you spot 10 differences between the two food displays?

Going Underground

It's daytime for these nature detectives, and the nocturnal animals are fast asleep.

Find **10** things that look different in these underground burrows.

Snowy Ride

Brr! It's a good day to wrap up warm!

Color in a paw print for each difference you find.

Spot **10** differences in the snowy scene below.

Computer Bug

Uh-oh, the tech teacher has never seen a computer bug like this before!

Find **10** differences
in the picture below.

Princess Puzzle

Circle **7** differences on the right half of this proud princess.

Robot Riddle

Find **6** differences on the right half
of this cheerful robot.

Toppings Trouble

Twins ordered exactly the same pizza, but the chef forgot some toppings on pizza 2!

Spot **10** differences in the pizza picture below.

Happy Heroes

These superfast sprinters took the medals at the World Jungle Games.

Start the clock! You have 2 minutes to find **14** differences between the pictures.

Drama Queen

Suzy Starr wants to be the world's most famous actress.

22

Look for **10** differences in this dressing room scene.

Tomb Raiders

Robbers have taken **10** treasures from the pharaoh's tomb.*

What's missing?

Monkey Puzzle

These sneaky monkeys have raided my backpack!

Spot the **9** differences on this page.

Under Attack

Raise the drawbridge! The castle
is under siege from a dragon!

Look for **11** things that have changed from the picture on the left.

Theater Trip

Today's performance is pretty spooky!
Spot **9** changes in the bottom picture.

30

Blast Off!

It's almost launch time! Find **10** differences before the rocket blasts off.

Dino Dig

Dig a little deeper to discover a dino skeleton!

Find **13** things that are different about the dino dig on this page.

33

Choose a Smoothie

Freddy goes batty for fruit smoothies!

Spot **10** differences in the picture below.

Lab Disaster

Fairground Ride

All the fun of the fair!

38

Find **14** differences on this page.

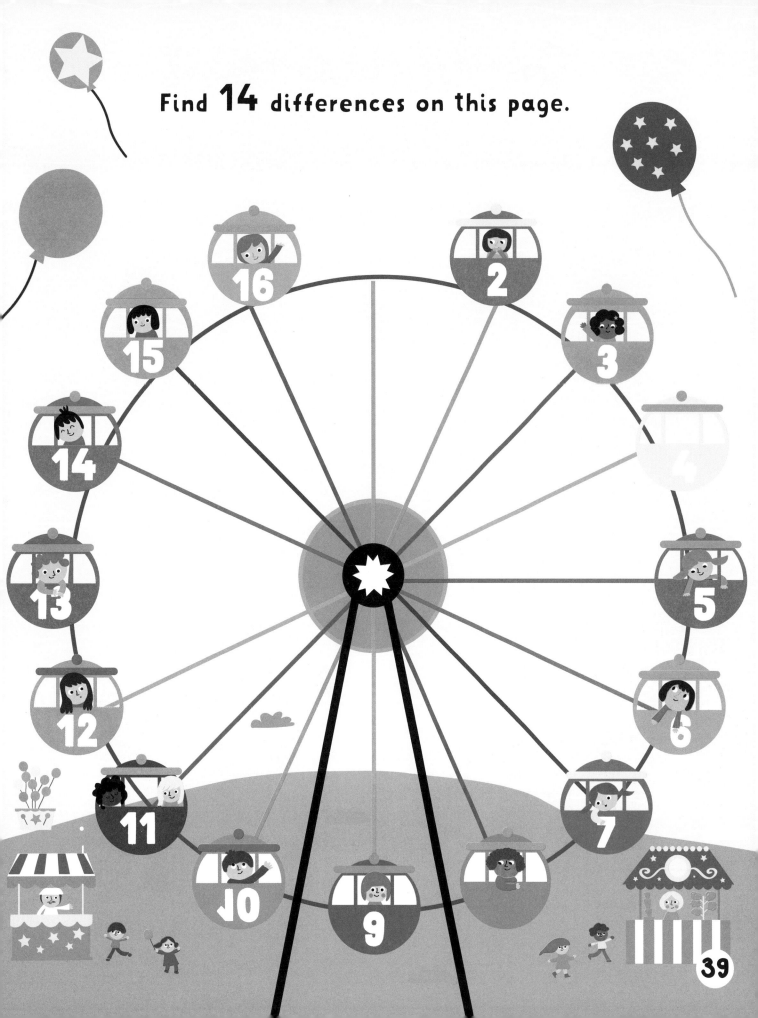

Butterfly Hunt

Beautiful butterflies – a treat for your eyes!

Spot **10** differences before they flutter on by.

Bird-watching

Which of these birds will fly south for the winter?

Circle the spaces where **10** birds have flown away.

Spare Seat?

Find **15** differences between the pictures of these busy buses.

Is there a spare seat for Sam?

Market Day

To market, to market...

Find **10** changes to this Roman market scene.

Different Dancers

Twirling and whirling, practicing for the big show!
Spot **11** differences in the bottom picture.

Parking Problem

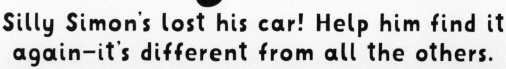

Silly Simon's lost his car! Help him find it again—it's different from all the others.

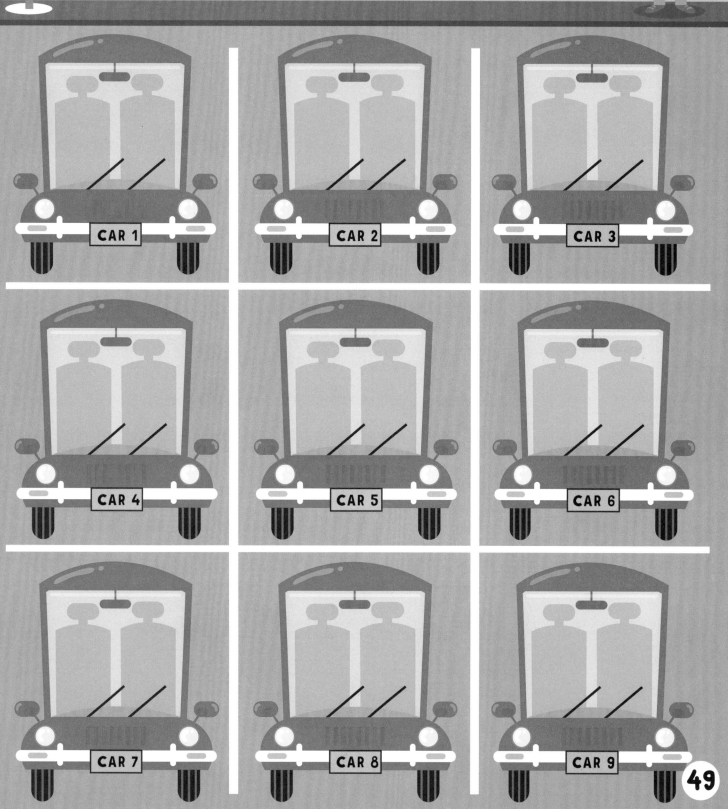

CAR 1
CAR 2
CAR 3
CAR 4
CAR 5
CAR 6
CAR 7
CAR 8
CAR 9

Down in the Jungle

Explore the jungle to discover some amazing animals.

Look for **12** things that have changed in the jungle scene below.

Night Owls

Hoot, hoot!

Can you see some owls acting differently? Spot **12** differences before dawn.

House Proud

DIY Dave is working on his dream home. Find **8** things he's updated in the picture below.

Different Ducks

Find **8** things that look different in the reflection of these feathered friends.

Hungry Whale

This big guy has a whale of an appetite,
but not everything is edible.

Spot **10** things that have been taken from his tummy to make the whale feel better.

Dragon Differences

This colorful Chinese dragon is ready for the New Year parade!

Busy Street

It's the morning rush on Main Street.

Can you find **15** differences on the busy street below?

Pirate Plunder

Here be treasure!
A chest of beautiful booty!

What's changed in this picture?
Spy **15** differences.

Greedy Giraffes

Look closely to spot **10** things that make us different.

I'm Gerry and this is Perry. We may be twins, but we're not exactly the same.

Bubble, Bubble

Willow the witch is stirring up something spooky.

Find **13** differences between the pictures or the witch will turn you into a toad!

Olivia's Outfits

Which outfit will Olivia wear today?
She has so many to choose from!

Her dresses are dry now, but some of them look different. Can you spot **12** changes?

Rocking Out!

The Rolling Rhinos are looking good and sounding wild!

Color in a guitar for each difference you find.

Build a Robot

Draw **5** things that are missing from the right side of Ratchet the robot.

Surf's Up

Turtle-y awesome!
Spot **10** differences
between the surf scenes.

On site

It's a strange day on site today. The builders keep finding all sorts of odd items!

74

Spot **15** strange things below that have appeared on site.

By the Beach

On sunny days these friends like to hit the beach.

What's changed? Color in a crab
for each difference you find.

Llama Drama

Check out these crazy creatures!

Find **14** differences between these funny farm scenes.

Temple Teaser

Professor Bones has discovered an ancient temple, but he has no idea what's written on the stones.

80

10 things have changed here. Study hard and spot them all.

ALien Eye-Spy

These aliens are keeping a close eye on the astronauts' visit to their planet.

Dive In!

What will you see under the sea?

Look for **10** things that are different here.

Snow Joke

Sensible and silly snowmen!
Spot **12** differences between them.

Strike!

Monkey's great at bowling! But will he get a strike or a spare? Circle **8** differences between the lanes.

Spotted!

Are you seeing spots?

There are **12** differences between these spotty scenes. Try to spot them all!

cake Bake

Hollie Hippo's cakes taste truly delicious!

Find **16** things that have changed in this kitchen picture.

Flour

Ramp It Up!

These champs of the ramps are trying out new tricks.

Get your skates on and find **16** changes.

93

Nest Test

It's dinnertime for these flying dinos.

94

Keep your eyes peeled for **16** differences.

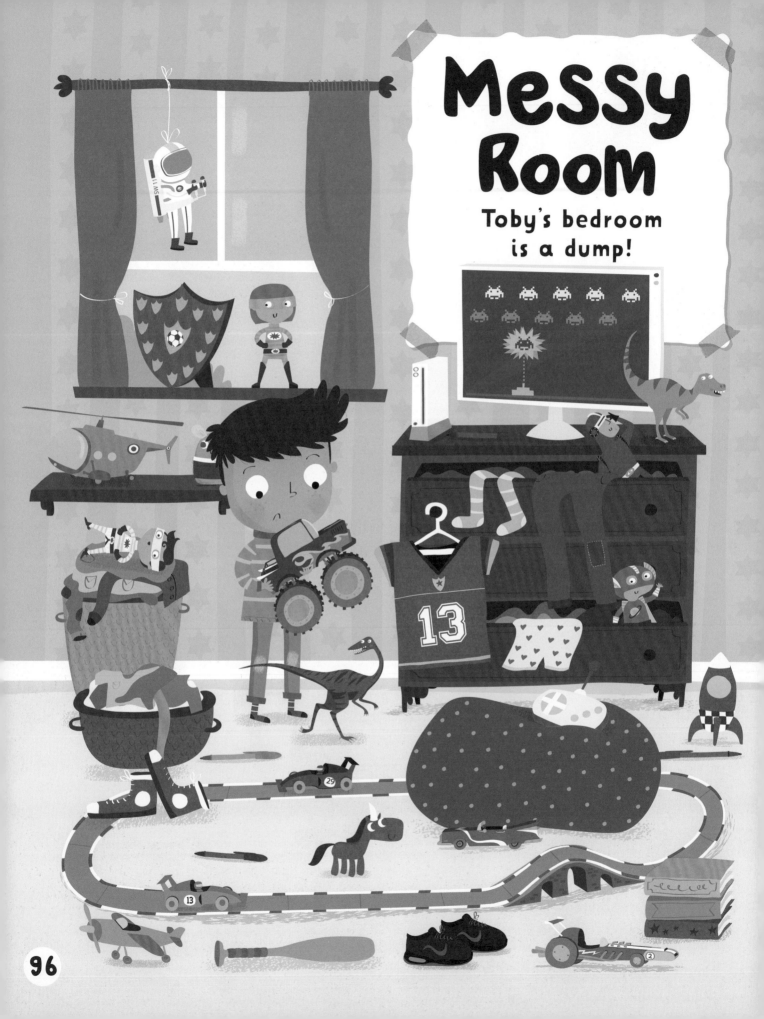

Messy Room

Toby's bedroom is a dump!

Circle **12** things that have changed in the bedroom below.

Something's fishy

Fish is the dish of the day!

8 things have changed in the bowl below. Find them all.

Setting sail

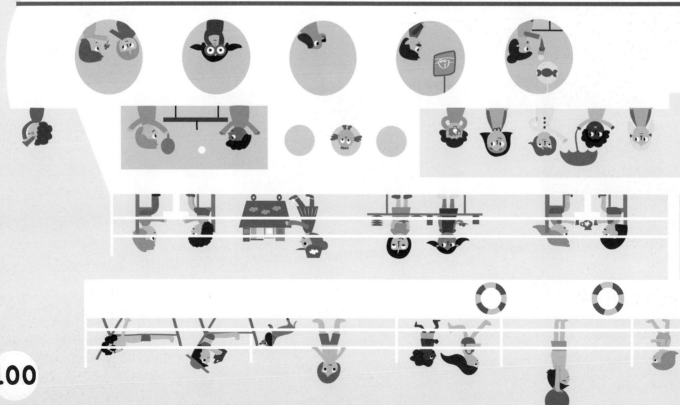

100

Castle Changes

Our castle needs some work to make it fit for royalty! Draw in **5** missing items on the right-hand side.

Boating Badgers

It's a race to the finish!

Discover **18** differences
between the pictures.

New 'do
Snip! Snip! Who wants a brand-new 'do?

Some things look different in the salon below. Can you spot **16** changes?

Teacher's Test

Pay attention, class! Here's a tricky test for you to try.

b c d e f g
h i j k l m n
o p q r
s t u v
w x y z

a b c d e f g h i j k l m n
o p q r s t u v w x y z

Meet Millie

Millie is sitting pretty. What's changed in the second picture? Circle **9** differences.

Slide Ride

It's snail's turn to ride the slide. Spot **9** differences on the right before he reaches the bottom.

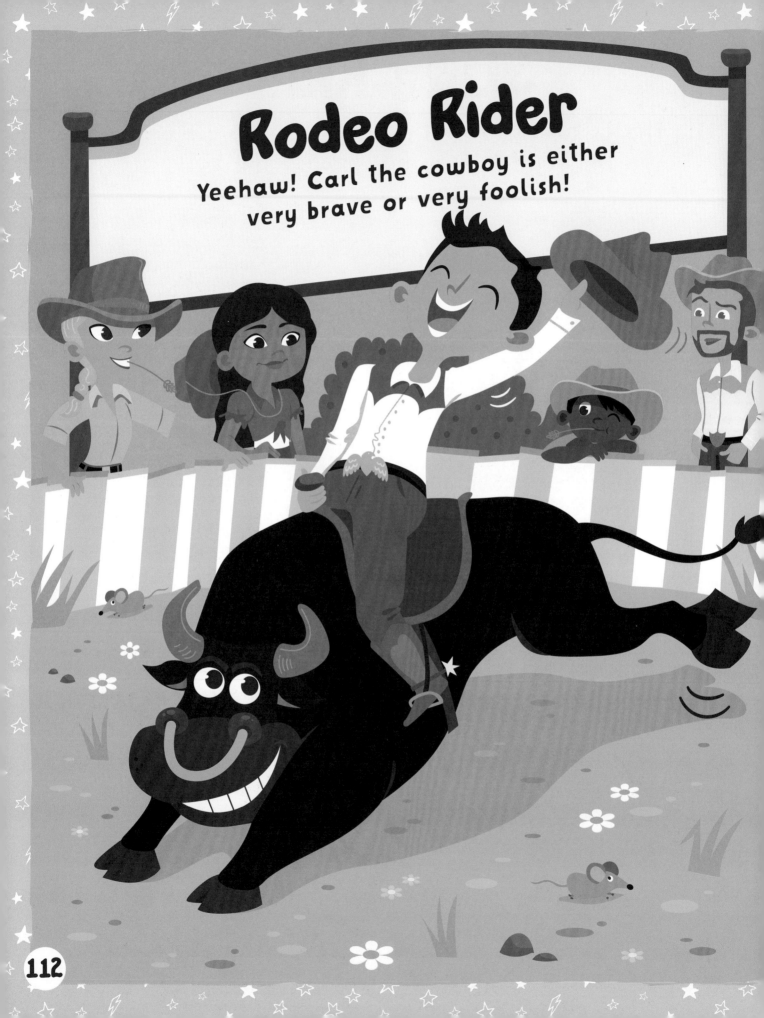

Rodeo Rider
Yeehaw! Carl the cowboy is either very brave or very foolish!

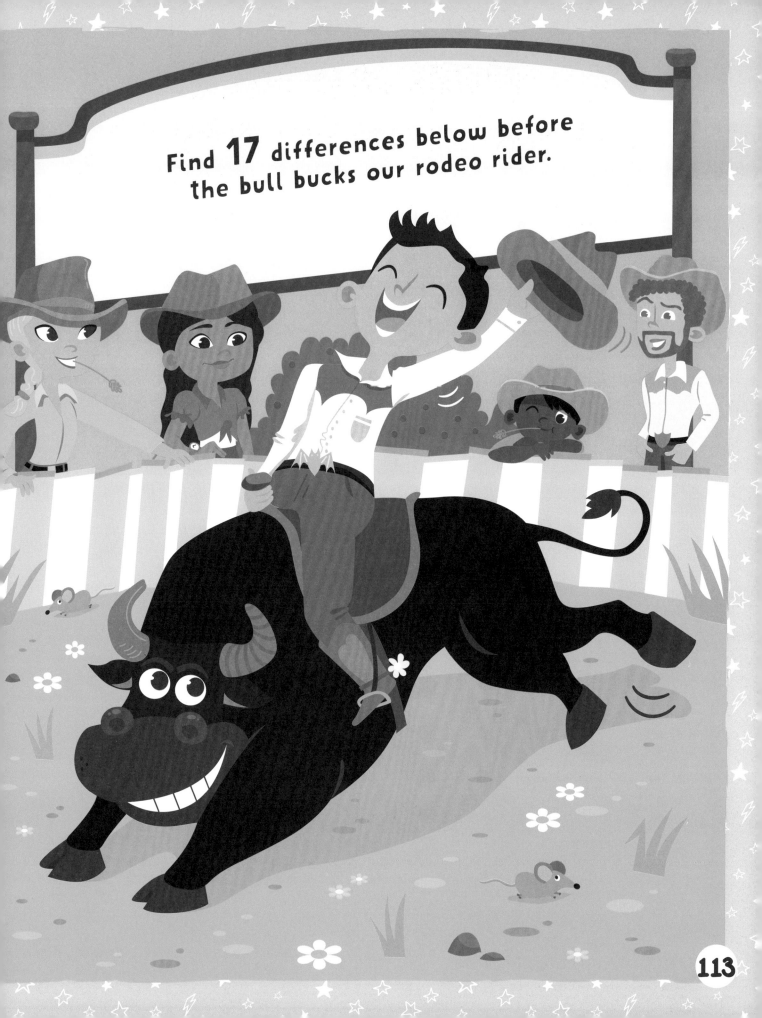

Find **17** differences below before the bull bucks our rodeo rider.

Map Muddle

Explorers are on an Aztec adventure!

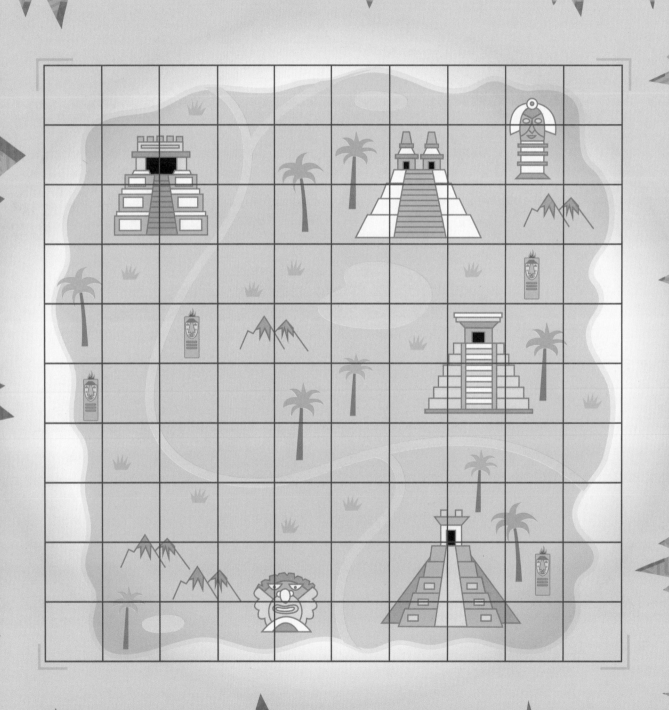

Study the maps and circle 8 things that have changed.

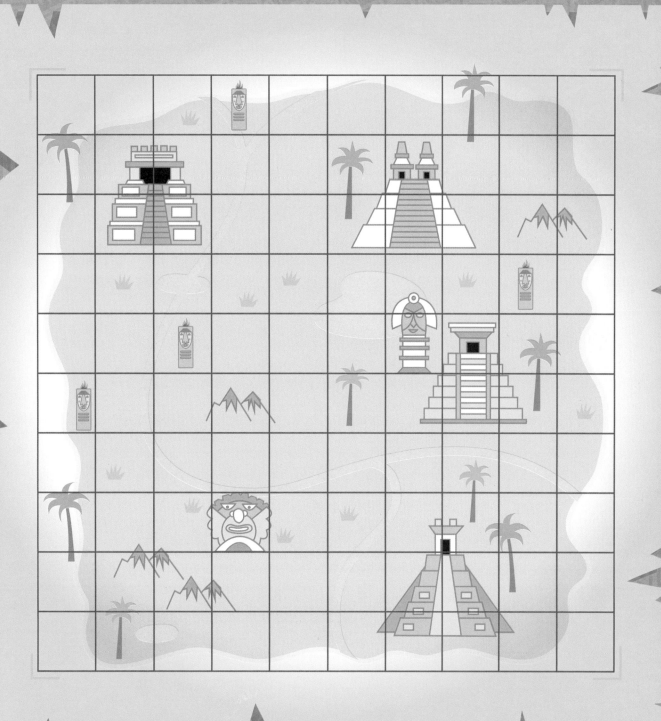

The Great Outdoors

The tent is up and the campfire is lit.
What could possibly go wrong?

Try to find **16** changes in the second scene.

Diner Dinner

A delicious dinner at the diner!

Look for **15** differences between the pictures.

119

Crafty Crooks

The midnight robbers have struck again!

Bling's Rings

Bling's Rings

12 things have changed in the picture below.
Spot them all before the crooks get **away!**

121

Answers

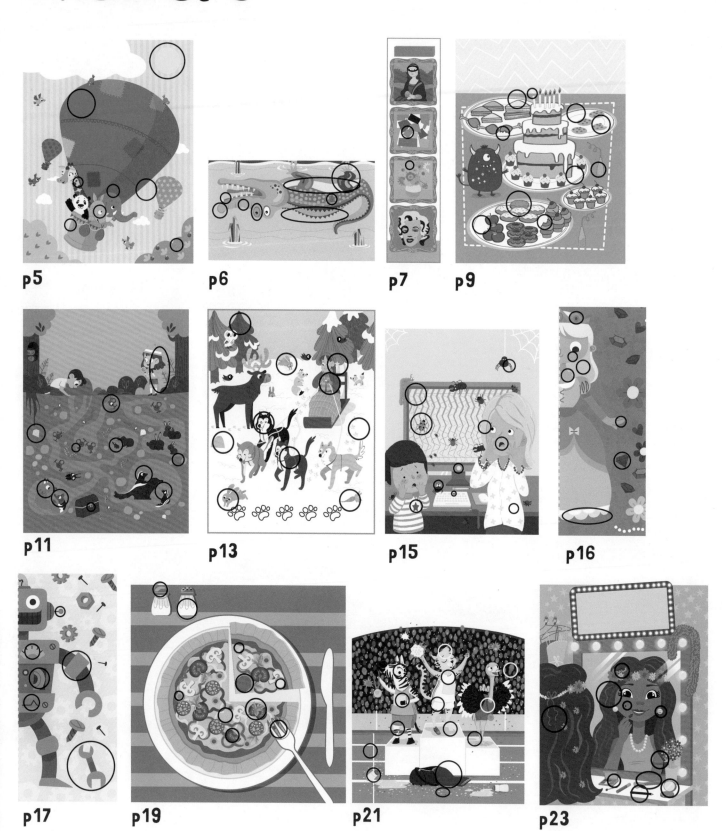

p5

p6

p7

p9

p11

p13

p15

p16

p17

p19

p21

p23

p25

p27

p29

p30

p31

p33

p35

p37

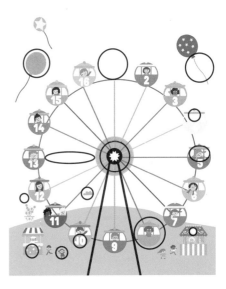

p39

p41

p43

p45

p47

p48

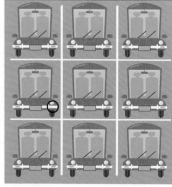

p49

p51

p53

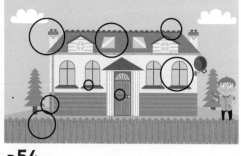

p54

p55

p57

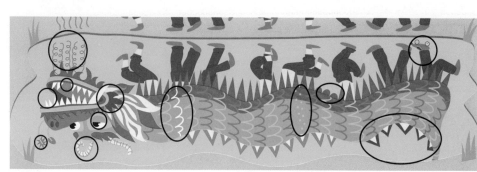

p59

p61

p63

p64-65

p67

p69

p71

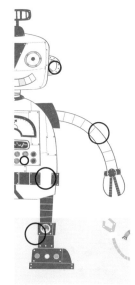

p72

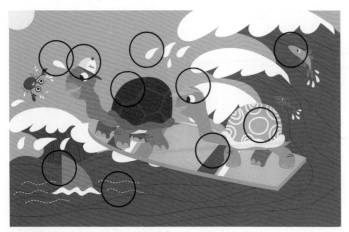

p73

p75

p77

p79

p81

p83

p85

p86

p87

p89

p91

p93

p95

p97

p99

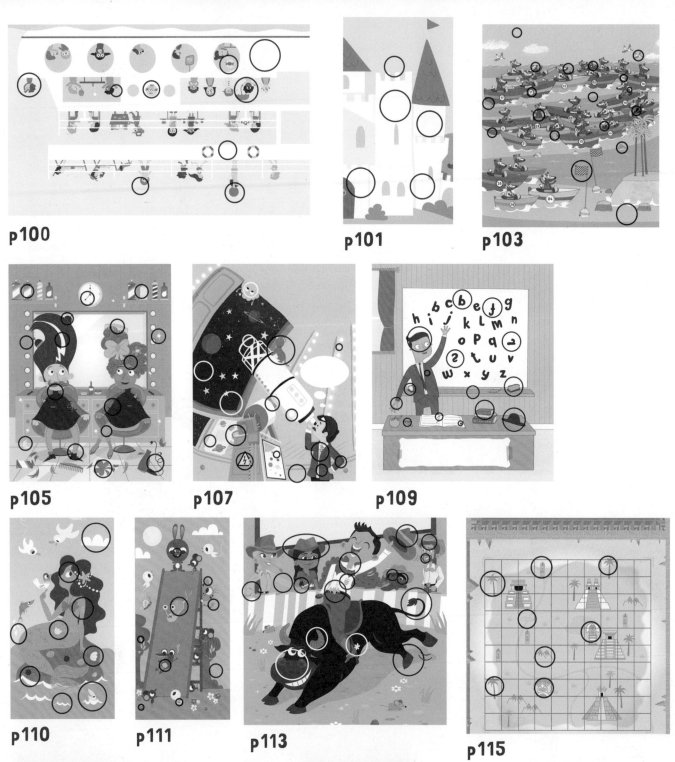

p100

p101

p103

p105

p107

p109

p110

p111

p113

p115

p117

p119

p121